Anna's Gift

THE
LATTER-DAY DAUGHTERS
S E R I E S

Anna's Gift
© 1995 by Carol Lynch Williams
All rights reserved.
Printed in the Untied States

No portion of this book may be reproduced in any form without
written permission from the publisher, Aspen Books, 6211 S. 380 W.,
Murray, UT 84107

Library of Congress Cataloging-in-Publication Data
Williams, Carol Lee Lynch.
Anna's Gift / by Carol Lynch Williams.
    p.   cm. — (Latter-day Daughters series ; 1)
Summary: While living in Nauvoo, Illinois, in the mid-nineteenth cen-
tury and enjoying the friendship of the Mormon prophet Joseph Smith, Anna
struggles to make her family see the importance of her gift for drawing.
        ISBN 1-56236-501-0 (alk. paper)
    [1. Artists—Fiction. 2. Mormons—Fiction. 3. Smith, Joseph,
    1805-1844—Fiction.] I. Title.   II. Series.
            PZ7.W65588An   1995
        [Fic]—dc20   95-15064
                                        CIP
                                        AC

10 9 8 7 6 5 4 3 2 1

Anna's Gift

T H E
LATTER-DAY DAUGHTERS
S E R I E S

Carol Lynch Williams

A S P E N
B O O K S

TABLE OF CONTENTS

Greater love hath no man than this, that
a man lay down his life for his friends.

JOHN 15:13

CHAPTER ONE

Drawing for the Prophet

"Anna, come skip rope with us," my friend Mary called to me. Mary was standing across the street with a group of girls from school.

"No thanks," I shouted back, waving, "I'm drawing." It made me feel good to say that so loudly. At home, Papa and Mama didn't like me to draw. But here, sitting on the wooden sidewalk, I felt free to do what I enjoyed so much. I sat watching some boys play marbles on the edge of the dusty street in front of me.

The sun beat down and for once I was glad I had my bonnet. Mama was always telling me to wear it but I couldn't see much use in keeping it on. Especially with weather so hot during summer days. Today, though, my bonnet shaded the paper and kept my dark brown hair out of my eyes.

I was trying to draw Jonathan, the boy who was marble champion, as he knelt in the circle. He was concentrating so hard I thought his face would make a good picture, freckles and all. Not bad, I thought when I was about half finished. I held the drawing away from myself a bit and smiled.

The door to the store behind me squeaked open and I covered my drawing by leaning over it. Jonathan stood up and rolling marbles around in his hand called, "Brother Joseph, play a game with us?"

The Prophet walked down the steps. "Hello, Anna," he said as he passed me. "How are you?"

"Fine, thank you." I smiled at him.

Brother Joseph turned his attention to Jonathan and the other boys. "I've left all my playing marbles at home."

"We'll loan you some," said another boy. The two boys' trousers* were dirty from kneeling on the ground.

Joseph Smith knelt in the circle, rubbed his hands together, and grinned.

"This is what I am needing," he said. "Some time to relax." The sun caught in his light colored hair, making it shine. He looked up once at me and winked. His eyes were so blue that for a minute I wished for paints or colored chalk to sketch with. What a picture it would be! I turned to a new piece of paper, even though I wasn't quite finished with the first, and began drawing the Prophet.

Each time a marble was sent spinning across the ring, the boys called out to each other in either excitement or disappointment.

"John, my granny can shoot better'n that and she's near blind in one eye," or "Oh no, three more of my marbles gone. I'm almost out of the game."

Brother Joseph laughed as he played.

Around us the streets buzzed with life. Horses neighed from where they were tied to posts. Someone from down the street called out about how hot it was. A cat ran past on the sidewalk, then cried to be let into the feedstore. I could hear the saw running at the mill not too far from town.

I sketched carefully as Brother Joseph moved his way around the circle, shooting marbles out of the ring that had been drawn into the ground with a stick.

"Joseph," called a man from across the way. "Won't be too much longer before we're judging the melons. I have one in my garden that looks like it'll have to be carried away in a cart, once it's time to move it! You got one you think will beat that?"

"Hard to say, Brother Peter. Only time will tell, but it sounds like you've got a winner."

Brother Peter laughed and wished the Prophet luck in his marble game.

The sun sparkled on the marbles making them glitter. At last Brother Joseph stood tall and handed the marbles he had won back to the boys.

"Good game," he said to them. "I look forward to another." He dusted off his knees and walked over to where I sat.

"Sister Robinson," he said, putting his hand out to me. I shook hands with him. "What have you here?"

Suddenly, I couldn't speak. Usually I found it very easy to talk to Brother Joseph. He was like a part of my family. He and Sister Emma visited with us often. They talked with Papa and Mama about things that were happening at church or how quickly the city was growing and who was moving in from where. No matter how busy he was Brother Joseph always made me feel I was as important as whatever was being talked about. He answered my questions. And before he would leave our home he would take both my sisters and me on his knee, one at a time.

He'd tell us to make sure Papa and Mama read the Book of Mormon to us every day. We knew Brother Joseph was teasing us about telling our parents what to do. That's what made it fun.

"I've been . . . uuum . . . drawing. I've been drawing . . . you." My voice could barely squeeze out of my throat. What if Brother Joseph told me I was frittering* away my time like Papa and Mama said? Or wasting my school paper? Had Papa talked to the Prophet already and told him I was not to draw? Embarrassed that I might be found guilty, I waited a few seconds before handing him my paper.

He looked at it and after a moment, smiled.

"You've a remarkable gift, Little One," he said, calling me the name Papa had given me because I had been such a tiny baby. "Would you mind doing one for me? I think Emma would like to have something like this."

"Oh, yes, Brother Joseph. I would love to draw for you." I couldn't believe it. He actually wanted me to draw. He said I had talent! I turned to a new page and began sketching another picture of the Prophet, feeling warm in the summer sun but warmer because of Brother Joseph's words.

"How is your mother, Anna?"

"She's doing well," I said. "She rests a lot."

"And have you been helping her?"

"Yes, sir," I said, looking at him closely. "I do most of the cleaning. And I help with the cooking, too. Papa says that my cornbread is beginning to taste as good as Mama's. With a little help I can make angel food cake. It's not perfect yet, but I keep trying to get it right."

"I'll have to visit some evening when I know you've been doing the baking," Brother Joseph said. "I am a pretty good judge of cakes, you know."

I laughed.

A stout, worried looking man came trotting through town on a big black mare. When he saw the Prophet sitting on the sidewalk, the man reigned to a halt. He climbed down from his horse and tethered it near the marble game. He hurried up to where Brother Joseph sat, pushing his way through the ring of boys. They mumbled a complaint at the interruption, but the man ignored them.

"Problems again last night," he said, sitting down heavily on the other side of Brother Joseph. He took a large kerchief from his pocket and mopped his red face with it. "Long after the wife and I settled in, I heard what sounded like wild animals coming from the direction of my fields. Kept on for the longest time. At first light I saddled up and rode out to the fields closest to our home, and sure enough, the crops had been destroyed. Trampled down to almost nothing."

I stopped drawing and my stomach turned cold. I knew the people of Illinois weren't happy about us being here. Our city was growing quickly. Papa said because Nauvoo was getting big so fast it made people in nearby cities nervous. I didn't understand, exactly, how it could be a bad thing to have so many of us here. Papa said some of it was because people thought we would all vote just how our church leaders told us to. But he said the true reason was because we were Mormons.

"They want the Prophet," I could almost hear Papa's words, low in the night to Mama. "They think if they stop Joseph Smith they will stop the Church." Papa called these men cowards because they worked when it was dark so no one could see them. Although the day was hot, I shivered at the thought.

"Is everything ruined, Brother Albert?" asked Brother Joseph.

"A lot of the fences are down and the wheat is gone."*

The Prophet sat quiet for a moment, then said,

"All will be well. At least for the time being. Go about your duties and have faith."

Brother Albert still looked worried. He let out a big sigh. "You're right, Brother Joseph. My wife is always telling me to have more faith." He stood then. "I guess I better get the flour and sugar she sent me after, or she'll be thinking I've taken a ride down the Mississippi on a riverboat."

We watched Brother Albert mount up and ride away, then Brother Joseph looked at me.

"Are you nearly finished, Anna?"

I shook my head no, trying not to show the fear that Brother Albert's words had left inside me.

"Would a story help ease your mind?" he asked.

I nodded, and with trembling fingers continued to work on the portrait. Brother Joseph began a story from the Book of Mormon. It was one that my family and I had read together many times. It was about Helaman and two thousand young men who were not much older than the boys who played marbles at our feet. The Prophet explained how all these young men had gone to fight for their parents. He described it all so perfectly that I was no longer afraid. Instead, I wanted to draw the pictures of the warriors marching to battle.

At last I handed my new sketch to Brother Joseph. He smiled at me and I was struck to the very heart by his kindness. How I loved our Prophet.

He stood, looking down at me. "This is wonderful, Sister Anna. I know Emma will like it. I'll tell her how hard you worked to give this gift to her." He helped me to my feet and then started away, speaking to the children who gathered around him.

"Wait," I called. "Wait, Brother Joseph." He turned back to me and I hurried up to him. "I forgot to put something on the picture. Can I have it back? I mean, may I?"

"Of course." He handed the drawing to me.

In the bottom right hand corner I wrote the date, June 20, 1844. Then I carefully signed my name, *Anna Robinson*, in my best script.*

"Thank you again," he said to me.

I watched him calling to everyone as he walked toward the Mansion House, laughing and happy. It made me feel good to see him that way.

I turned, then, and ran for home, my heart thumping. I had drawn the prophet! Oh, how I wished I could share my news.

CHAPTER TWO

Charlette Tells

"You're in trouble," Charlette said to me when I came into the fenced yard. I ignored her. Charlette, who was eight, two years younger than me, sat waiting on the front steps of our red brick house. She was always spying on me. I couldn't think that my being gone for a little while had changed anything.

I held my paper close and walked through the parlor and then up the stairs to the bedroom I shared with my sisters. I hid my things in the clothes press,* behind my Sunday dress. I closed the door until it clicked shut, then turned around.

Charlette had snuck up behind me! She and Sidnie, our little sister, were standing quiet inside our bedroom. They were holding hands and looked almost like twins. Both of them have hair as light as corn silk.

It's so curly that a comb will hardly go through it. They stared at me with brown eyes, the color of our rich garden soil. Then Charlette tried to look into the clothes press that I was standing in front of.

"What are you hiding?" she asked. "What did you put in there?" Then she drew in a deep breath. "Why Anna, you've been drawing again. I saw the paper you were carrying."

Sidnie stood quiet, sucking her thumb.

"Don't do that, Sidnie," I said, acting as though I hadn't heard a word from Charlette. "Mama doesn't like it when you suck your thumb." Sidnie slowly pulled her thumb from her mouth.

"I'm telling Mama, Anna." Charlette's voice buzzed like an angry mosquito.

I went to Sidnie and knelt in front of her. I smoothed her tangled hair away from her forehead, then kissed her.

"Anna?" Charlette's tone was a warning. I knew it wouldn't be long before she was off down the hall to tell Mama everything she thought I had done. I had to think of something to tell her fast.

"I put an old frog in your dress pocket," I said, looking up from where I knelt. "You can't see it yet, because it's so small, but it's gonna start growing.

Then you'll feel it moving around, right in the middle of Sunday sermon. It'll start croaking right when the sacrament cup* is passed to you. Now . . ." I stood and leaned close into Charlette's face, and she backed away a little, "quit following me. Just let me alone, or you'll be sorry sure."

Sidnie was swallowing hard. Her eyes were huge. She started to put her thumb into her mouth, but instead sucked on her bottom lip. Charlette looked at me wide-eyed too, blinking fast, as though she was trying not to cry. Then after a second she said:

"I'm telling Mama that you're trying to scare us. You know she says you're not to tell us tales. She says it makes it hard for Sidnie to sleep when you fill her mind with such nonsense."

I rolled my eyes at Charlette. "You're sounding like an old school marm." I flounced around the room acting as if I was wearing a dress with lots of petticoats. Then I pretended I was looking through a pair of spectacles* at Charlette. I pinched my lips together exactly as she did whenever she acted better than me.

"Stop that, Anna. You're being so mean." Charlette turned to Sidnie. "Don't you worry, there's no such thing as frogs like what she's saying."

Charlette jerked her thumb in my direction.

"On the banks of the Mississippi you never know what you'll find," I said. Then ignoring Charlette, I looked at Sidnie. "How's Mama doing?"

"Her's resting," said Sidnie. "Her says it's too hot to do anything. Her says her hopes no neighbors show up."

"Ribbit," I said in my most froglike voice and I pushed past Charlette. "Stay here while I look in on Mama."

I walked down the hall to Mama and Papa's room. The door was open to allow a breeze to blow through. But today there was no breeze anywhere in Nauvoo, I was sure of that.

Mama was lying on the bed, fully dressed, her hands resting on her big stomach. I took the cloth that covered her eyes and wet it again in the water in the blue-flowered wash basin. I put it gently on her face. Her light brown hair, coming a little loose from its bun, lay smoothly on the white pillow.

"Oh, Anna," she said to me. Her voice was soft. Since the moment Mama had discovered she was going to have a baby everything about her turned soft, her voice, her ways, her walk. Mama didn't do the chores that she used to. She just rested, hoping she wouldn't have to bury another baby. She had told Papa, late one night when I was supposed to be sleeping, that burying a fourth baby would be the death of her.

"You help me so much, Anna."

I felt guilty for a moment. I had done all my chores before running off to draw that morning, but I hadn't taken Charlette and Sidnie with me when I left. I couldn't unless I wanted everyone in town to know that I was going against the wishes of my papa and mama by drawing. I tried to brush away my guilt as I would the flies that buzzed at the dinner table.

"What can I get for you, Mama?"

"Nothing," she said. "I'm just resting. What have you been doing this afternoon?"

"Not too much," I said. It was true. I had only drawn. "But I did talk to Brother Joseph."

Mama uncovered her eyes when I mentioned the Prophet.

"How is he?" she asked.

I told her almost all that had happened that afternoon: About him playing marbles and talking with me at length. I kept quiet about Brother Albert's fields and my drawing. No need to get Mama too worried. I told her about all the little things that made up my time in town: some of the conversations I had heard, the people who asked about her, what I saw in the milliner's* window. I knew Mama missed getting out and talking with her friends. And I knew she missed the visits of Brother Joseph and Sister Emma. It seemed each time they came lately they stayed only a short while on account of Mama resting.

"She's been out drawing again," Charlette said, poking her head in at the door. "I saw her trying to hide her paper. Then she started telling tales about how she was going to . . . "

That little sneak was peeping in at Mama and me! I turned around fast, but Charlette ran away down the hall. She didn't even finish her sentence.

"Have you been drawing?" Mama asked me, her voice terrible because it was so quiet.

"Yes ma'am," I said, bowing my head.

"On your school paper again?"

"Yes, Mama." It was a whisper of an answer.

"What am I to do with you?" Mama asked. With a heavy sigh, she sat up. "There's dinner to get ready before Papa gets home, Anna. Can I trust you to help me?"

"Of course, Mama," I said, and we went downstairs together.

CHAPTER THREE

My Punishment

Papa came in from work hot and tired. There was wood dust in his reddish-brown beard and even in his eyebrows. "The temple's coming along just fine, Lydia," he told Mama while we were eating dinner. Papa had been doing carpentry work there today, as he did every tenth day—tithing his time. All able-bodied people in Nauvoo helped. It was an honor to work on the temple.* "The sisters have been asking about you. I've told them you're doing well—that you're resting." Papa turned to me. "little one, have you been helping?"

"Yes, Papa," I said. But before I could say any more Charlette interrupted.

"Papa," she said. "Ask Anna what she drew today when she went into town." Charlette said this with a sweet smile on her face. Then she turned to me, squinched her eyes closed, and wrinkled her nose.

I was so angry, I wanted to slap that smile right off Charlette's face. I was surprised I felt so mad. It was wrong to feel this way because I *had* been drawing again. And against Papa's will. But why wasn't Charlette's running to Mama good enough? Why did she have to tell Papa, too?

"Anna," Papa said, putting down his fork. "You've been drawing when I've forbidden it?"

I nodded without looking at him. "Yes, Papa."

"I thought we talked about this before." Papa's voice was stern.

"Yes, sir."

"Don't you understand? There are chores to be done here. Your Mama needs looking after, to keep up her strength. I don't want her getting too tired. It's not that much longer before this baby blesses our home. You promised me that you wouldn't draw when you're needed here so badly."

"But Papa," I said. "I waited until all my chores were done before I left . . ." I glared at Charlette, then looked back at Papa, my face burning with shame. "I'm sorry. It's just . . . Papa, I love drawing so much. I didn't think there'd be any harm in my doing a little sketching if I had done all my chores first." There was no use trying to explain. I couldn't say rightly what I felt inside.

"You made a vow, Anna," Papa said, "and then broke it. That's where the harm lies. How can I trust you? When we Robinsons make a promise, we keep it. We stand by our words."

I nodded, hurt to the very center because I had disappointed Papa and Mama. And hurt that I wouldn't be able to draw anymore. Out of the corner of my eye I could see Charlette trying to hide a smile behind her hand.

"It won't happen again," I said, my voice nearly a whisper. I wanted to tell Papa what Brother Joseph had said about how good I was at drawing, how he wanted me to sketch his portrait. But that would be causing trouble. In my heart I promised that I would do everything that Papa and Mama needed me to do. And no matter how badly I wanted to, I wouldn't draw.

There was a hard look in Papa's brown eyes. "And as for you Charlette Robinson. You've become an eight-year-old gossip hen. I don't want to hear any more words against your sister. Do you understand?"

"Yes, Papa," Charlette said. Her voice was low.

I wanted to grin at my sister, to poke fun at her now that *she* was in trouble, but my heart felt heavy.

I had gone against what Papa wanted. I had to accept my punishment, whatever it might be.

"Anna," Papa said after a few minutes of silence. "If your Mama were up to it I'd have her watch over you all day, as though you were a newly born baby again, to make sure that you were doing all I told you to. Or told you not to. But I have to try trusting you again. I expect my girls to choose the right way."

I nodded my head, without looking Papa in the eye.

"What about me, Papa?" asked Sidnie, suddenly. There was gravy running down her chin and she was wearing a moustache of milk.

He laughed.

"Come here, little angel," he said.

Sidnie ran around the table to Papa, her curly hair haloing her face like a soft yellow cloud. She threw herself into his lap. He pulled her close to him and for a moment I was jealous. It seemed three was the right age to be.

CHAPTER FOUR

Getting Back at Charlette

As soon as I promised Papa that I would never draw again, everything I looked at needed drawing. Why, I thought, a picture of Charlette frowning because she had gotten in trouble would make people laugh until they cried. Mama with her feet up, biding her time, was another sketch.

The hens and biddies pecking up the leftover bits of food would make a good picture.

And when I stared at myself in our looking glass, and my dark blue eyes stared back, angry at my sister, I thought that would be a good drawing, too. If I could only catch the way I felt and put it down on paper. My fingers itched to try.

The feeling was worse that night as I lay in bed, hot between Sidnie and Charlette, who both snuggled close to me. That's when I started thinking about the story Brother Joseph had told me. I could see

Helaman again. He was sitting up high on his horse. The title of liberty banner was waving in the wind. Helaman, big and strong, was leading the young boys to war against the evil Lamanites. That just had to be drawn.

Why not sneak into the clothes press and get my paper? Sidnie was breathing deeply and soon Charlette would be, too. No one would ever know. The thought made me sit up in bed. As quickly as this thought of drawing came into my mind, another popped up right next to it. It wasn't true that no one would know. I would.

"Why did you have to tell, Sister Busybody?" I hissed at Charlette. When she didn't answer, I sighed. I couldn't even argue with her about it to make myself feel better.

I crawled out of bed and went and stood in the square of moonlight that puddled onto our bedroom floor. I rested my arms on the window sill and looked out past the tall chestnut tree to the temple. It stood white on the hill.

It wasn't fair. It just wasn't fair. Suddenly, I thought I knew how it was to be locked up with no freedoms. And it was all Charlette's fault. I had to get back at her. I just had to. I looked out the window for a long while. Finally I came up with an idea. Why not make my frog threat come true?

And just my luck, Sunday was only two days away.

Sunday morning early, before anyone was awake, I got out of bed without making a sound. I changed into my oldest dress, one that was too short for me and tight in the shoulders. Once outside, I grabbed the milk bucket and raced down to the Mississippi.

The full moon was low and yellow in the dark sky, lighting my way. As I ran out of town toward the river, I was grateful that we weren't too far from its banks. What I was doing was a little scary. I mean being out all by myself this early in the morning. And Mama had warned me plenty of times that I was never to go into the water alone because I would drown sure. I could swim, just not very well.

But I wasn't going to get into the water. Just look around near it.

By the time I was close to the river's edge, I was wishing that I was a champion swimmer. Whew! The weather was hot and sticky—even this early in the morning. Especially in the swampy areas where mosquitoes buzzed. As I walked through the low bushes, I thought of filling the milk bucket I was carrying with water, then dumping it over my head to cool myself off. I would have done it, too, except how could I explain being all wet once I snuck back into our house?

The sight that greeted me was enough to make me break my vow to Papa. The river stretched out wide and the moon sliced it into parts with its light, wavering and dancing on the currents. The trees on the opposite bank were black silhouettes against the lighter sky that was filled with weakening stars. It was as if they knew the sun was on its way back into the sky. Something was stuck in the water, an old log or branch, and sitting in the moon's ray on the wood was a great heron. How I wished for my drawing paper and pencil.

Around me lightning bugs flickered. Crickets and frogs sang to the river. I slapped at mosquitoes. But mostly I just looked at the water, the reflections, the trees black on the opposite bank, and that beautiful bird. I had to squeeze my hands tight to make the drawing urge go away. This feeling gave me courage to poke around looking for frogs so that I

23

could get back at Charlette. I knew I ran a chance of meeting up with a nest of water moccasins.* The thought sent shivers all over my bare arms and legs.

With an effort I looked away from the river into the marshes and started trying to find a frog. I had to hurry. It wouldn't be much more than an hour before Papa would be getting up to tend the animals.

I splashed through the low lying water trying to follow croaking sounds. Whenever I got near the frogs though, everything became quiet. Sometimes I could hear them jumping away. But I could never get close enough to any one frog to lay my hands on it.

Finally I saw a whole frog family, their bulging eyes watching me make my way quietly toward

them. Some were huge, as big as a small cat, and green like the weeds around them. Some were speckled with brown, their skins smooth and wet. As I moved slowly toward one that looked to be the papa, a streak of fear, like ice, ran through my stomach. I could *see* the frog. I could see his colors, his very eyeballs, gold and black.

The sun was up! Suddenly the frog didn't seem so important.

I fell three times running home, once in green

scum hiding a wide, shallow puddle of water. The milk pail banged against me as I ran. I thought of throwing it in the bushes and coming back for it later, but I knew I'd catch more trouble for that. Branches grabbed at me, pulling at my dress and scratching my legs, slowing me down. I knew it was already too late to beat anyone awake.

As my feet pounded on the dirt street, they seemed to drum out the words, "Trou-ble, trou-ble, trou-ble." Home never seemed so far away. But it was still too close to give me time to come up with a good excuse for leaving so early on the Sabbath—without permission—and coming back filthy.

CHAPTER FIVE

Mobs

When I walked into the kitchen Mama sat down quickly, then said, "Go stop your father. He's in the barn getting ready to go looking for you." I walked slowly outside.

"Papa?" I called when I got to the barn door.

He turned from saddling Midnight. "Anna!" Papa was dressed for church, in his black pants and coat and white high-collared shirt. His mouth dropped open when he saw how dirty I was. Relief washed over his face and then anger. "Where have you been, girl? What have you been doing?"

"I've been down to the river."

"The river?" Papa's voice was loud. "What deviltry were you about at the river? We've told you time and again the dangers that lurk there."

"I know, Papa," I said. "It was just . . ." I

straightened my shoulders and looked right at him. I would tell him the whole truth. "I was trying to find a frog."

"A frog?"

I spoke really fast. "Papa, every time I turn my back, Charlette's sneaking up on me so she can run lickity split back to you and Mama to tell on me. I wanted to make her leave me alone. I thought if I put a frog in her church dress pocket . . ." I shrugged my shoulders.

"You thought she wouldn't tell us you had done that?"

"Well, I knew she would tell you, but I thought it would be so funny I wouldn't mind much when she did. And it would do her good, seeing all the calamity she's caused me."

Papa laughed right out loud and I was surprised. Then he grew solemn. "Didn't you think of the consequences of a frog at church? How do you think President Richards would feel? Or the other Saints? And us being such good friends with the Prophet. My children should be obedient as an example to the others that go to our meetings." He put his hand on my shoulder. It felt warm and strong.

I hung my head, feeling ashamed again. I hadn't

really thought of the commotion a frog might cause. I wanted to smile thinking about it but decided it was best not to.

"You go and explain this to Mama," Papa said with a sigh. "Of all the things that you did, the fear you put in your mother's heart is what I'm most vexed about."

"Yes, Papa."

"And Anna, did you give cause to think what might have happened to you if you had slipped into the river and been dragged downstream? You've heard the paddleboats firing cannons* into the water. You know what that's for."

I nodded. I had stood on the banks before and watched the big boats fire into the river for somebody feared to have drowned. The shots were supposed to make the dead person float to the top of the water.

"How would it have been for your Mama to lose you after your three brothers?"

"I'm sorry, Papa."

Papa and I were quiet. He squeezed my shoulder, then turned and started unsaddling Midnight.

"Mama and I are going to talk things over. We need to determine what must be done about this naughty behavior. I cannot permit you to be grieving your mother anymore after what she has been through today. It can't be good for her or that baby. Now go get ready for church."

I started for the house. As quickly as I could, I cleaned up. Standing in the wash tub* I poured cold water through my hair and over my dirty arms and legs. There wasn't time to heat water on the stove. The mud was dried now and hard to remove. I had to scrub till my skin turned pink.

At last, I put on my blue Sunday dress, stockings, and button-up shoes. I combed out my dark hair and saved the strands that caught in the comb* in a small wooden box that sat near the wash basin. Later, when I had enough, I would embroider something with the hair. Maybe a simple line sketch. Or was that too much like drawing? Would Papa and Mama consider that breaking my promise to them? I plaited* my waist-length hair and tied a Sunday ribbon around the end. I ran down the stairs.

"It's the Sabbath, Anna," Mama said softly from where she was sitting at the table. I slowed to a walk. "Have you something to say to me?" she asked.

I nodded and told her the same story I had told my father. I left out everything about really wanting to be an artist. I knew that Mama wouldn't understand that. There was just too much to be done around home: staking out our cow, Betsy, and her calves, Hi and Lo; bringing in water for the day; sweeping; weeding the garden; gathering eggs, and taking care of my sisters.

"I was sorely grieved when I awoke this morning and couldn't find you. I want to be able to speak well of my oldest daughter," Mama said. "I can't if she is a disobedient child."

I felt my cheeks flush.

"Yes, ma'am." I was so embarrassed that I wished I could slip between the cracks in the kitchen floor. Mama's corrections were always more stinging than Papa's.

"Take some biscuits from that covered pan on the shelf for your breakfast. I've already filled them with honey. And don't forget the blanket. We must leave." Mama smoothed her brown wool dress as though she was feeling for wrinkles. Even in her hot clothes, Mama looked cool.

I took hold of her hand as we walked out the door to where Papa and Charlette and Sidnie were waiting for us. We started down the road to the Grove. Mama was humming softly under her breath.

From the distance we saw a horse and rider coming quickly up the street, raising dust high into the air. When the rider got closer I saw that it was Brother Samuel McAllister.

"Brother John," he said to Papa, "I must speak with you. Privately. Excuse me, Sister Lydia." Brother Samuel bowed his head slightly to Mama, touching the brim of his hat with his fingertips.

Papa and Brother Samuel walked off down the road, trailing the horse behind them. They moved back toward our home. Mama and the rest of us continued on to our meetings, but, oh, I was itching to hear what news Brother Samuel had brought with him.

After a few minutes, Brother Samuel climbed up on his horse and started off fast in another direction. Papa caught up with us.

"Lydia," he said, "a mob burned a couple of the wheat fields on the north side of town."

CHAPTER SIX

Being Afraid

I thought Mama was going to faint. Her face went pale and she nearly fell onto me. "No!" Mama said. "Not again. Not here."

Papa moved forward quick and held Mama up. "Come back home, Lydia. You need rest after the scare you've had this morning." Papa glanced over at me.

I cringed inside but stood still and waited to see what he wanted us to do.

"Go on ahead to the Grove, Anna," Papa said. His voice was tired. "Take your sisters with you. I'll be along shortly. And mind, you three behave." I knew Papa was worried, not just about Mama but about the fields. And so was I.

I thought of Brother Albert and what he had talked about when I was sketching Brother Joseph's picture. I wondered if Papa knew that Brother Albert's wheat had been destroyed, too.

We walked to the small grove of trees near the temple where we met for Sunday meetings when the weather was nice. Some people carried chairs from home, and there were tree stumps to sit on, but I carried a blanket to spread on the ground on the women's side. We were early enough that we had pretty good seats. At least we would be able to hear what was said if the speaker talked good and loud.

When Papa arrived, he sat on the grass with the men. He waved to the three of us and I could tell that he wasn't upset with me.

I looked for Brother Joseph but couldn't see him anywhere. I tried to guess who would speak to us today, as so many of the Apostles were away on missions. I looked again at Papa. His head was bowed. I wondered at all his worry.

Suddenly I was struck with guilt at what I had done just that morning. I had caused Mama grief. I had gone to a place I was forbidden to go. I had played on the Sabbath. How could I do such things when I really wanted to be helping out Papa and Mama?

My heart ached. I prayed, hoping to ease my burden. Hot tears filled my eyes. I squeezed them shut. I didn't want to cry here in front of everyone.

I turned my thoughts to the burning fields. When had this happened? Was Papa so worried about where I was that he hadn't even known the city's crops were being destroyed by angry people? And what was going to happen next? Would it be the same as it had been in Kirtland, Ohio? We had already lost the city that was supposed to be the true gathering place for all God's Saints. Would mobs try to drive us from Nauvoo, too? Our Temple was only half built.

I felt afraid and sad. My stomach churned, heavy with the biscuits and honey I had eaten so quickly on the way. I was frightened with the thoughts of being driven from another home.

The trip from Kirtland had been hard. Mama's baby hadn't lived but a few hours after being born in a wagon one starless night. I had held Mama's hand until Sister Eliza sent me off to be with Papa and Charlette, saying a six-year-old had no business being with her mama during a time like this. I left her side only because she had nodded for me to go.

Later we buried my baby brother, so tiny and still. And Mama cried like I never remembered her crying before. Like I've never heard her cry since. Not even when we buried the twin boys did Mama cry as she did on the trail. Maybe because now she thought we were safe.

But we couldn't be safe if the fields were being trampled and burned. We couldn't be safe if mobs were threatening again. I closed my eyes tight and asked Heavenly Father to bless Mama and to watch over the Saints here in Zion.

We hurried home after meetings to eat dinner. I milked the cow and then carried the fresh milk into the cellar to keep cool. I looked at our backyard garden with pride. It was growing well. Beans and peas pushed their way through the dark soil. Melons were growing thick and heavy on sturdy vines, the green balls promising sweet red fruit. In the heat of that Sunday afternoon I dreamed of cutting one of the big melons open and eating it right there in the garden. I could almost feel the juice dripping down my chin and running down my arms.

Later, I sat with Charlette and Sidnie, quiet in the yard, under the chestnut tree where it was a little bit cooler.

"We're getting too old to be fussing so much at each other," I said. "We need to be loving and kind and try to do what we learned today in our church meeting. Remember what Brother Richards said about doing kind things for other people? He said Jesus had the greatest love because He died for his friends."

"Yes, Anna," said Charlette with a sigh. "I remember. I was listening, you know."

"I was listening real hard, too," said Sidnie. She wrapped and unwrapped a cloth doll in the nine-patch quilt* I had made just last year. Every once in a while she would hold the doll up to her shoulder and pat it gently on the back.

I hugged Sidnie up close to me. "Mama needs us to be 'specially good," I said to Charlette. "This baby is really important to her." I was quiet for a minute. "And it's important to me, too."

For once Charlette wasn't prissy. "I want the baby here, too," she said.

We all sat in silence, me wondering just how much Charlette could remember of our brothers that died.

Monday was quiet, with Papa worried because three more fields were burned by the mobs. It puzzled me to know that some of these angry men were people who had once been Brother Joseph's friends. It scared me to think how easy it was to turn against someone important to you. Turn far enough that you didn't care whether you hurt another person or not.

I had to be brave. Since I was the oldest, I couldn't let anyone know I was afraid. Least of all Charlette and Sidnie. I needed to set the example, Papa and Mama were always telling me that.

Tuesday afternoon brought us worrisome news. I was weeding in the garden before it got too hot to work when I saw Papa coming down the road. He was walking fast, almost running. I stood up. I wanted to go out into the road and meet him, but I didn't. I just stood still with weeds in my hand, their bitter smells strong.

"Papa," I said, when he was close enough to hear. "Why aren't you at at work? It's not dinner time."

"Keep on pulling weeds, little one," he said to me. As he walked into the house I heard him call, "Lydia?" Papa's voice was troubled and it caused fear in my heart. Here I was promising myself not to be afraid and I was so scared I was having a hard time swallowing. My throat was all dry, as if I'd been eating the dirt, not working in it.

Why was Papa home? Had more fields been burned? Maybe someone's barn? Or a house? It took all my efforts to stay in the garden, then to make my knees bend and to keep pulling weeds from the crumbly earth. I wished I was Charlette, cleaning in the kitchen, just long enough to hear what Papa was telling Mama.

But Papa sent Charlette out back to help me.

"You didn't hear anything?" I asked Charlette when she knelt in the dirt.

"No. I tried to listen at the door to the parlor and Papa sent me out here quick like that." Charlette snapped her fingers.

After a few minutes Papa came hurrying out of the house and went off without a word to us. It was almost as if he didn't see us there between the rows of radishes and carrots, watching him. Then he was late for supper, but Mama wouldn't let any of us eat until he came home.

"He's on important business," was all she said, looking out the back door often, watching for Papa. When she saw him riding up on our horse, Midnight, she said, "Set the food on the table quickly, Anna." Then she sat down and waited.

After the blessing on the food, Papa smiled at

Mama and said, "We raised the money for the bail. Brother James and a couple of other men are riding hard to Carthage today." Papa laughed quietly. "They didn't think we could do it. But we did. With God's help we managed it."

"Managed what, Papa?" I asked at last. I knew I should sit quietly, but I just couldn't.

"You have a right to know what's happening," Papa said. Then he took a big breath. "This morning the guns from the Nauvoo Legion were handed over to the state."

My heart started beating hard. The Nauvoo Legion was our very own army, organized by the Prophet. How could we be protected if there were no guns?

"What do you mean by bail, Papa?" Charlette asked.

"Bail is when you raise money to get someone out of jail."

"You mean someone is in jail? But I thought they just took our guns," I said, feeling confused. "Do you have to buy them back?"

Papa cleared his throat. "No. I don't think we'll be getting them back any time soon. The bail was for the Prophet. You see, Brothers Joseph and Hyrum were imprisoned today, along with John Taylor and Doctor Richards. A few others, too, but the sheriff's letting some of them come on back home."

I didn't think I could eat, even knowing that the money had been raised for bail.

Papa kept on talking, trying not to smile, "So they set the bail high, thinking we couldn't raise the 7,500 dollars."

"Seven thousand, five hundred dollars!" Charlette said. "That's so much."

Charlette was right, it was a huge amount of money.*

"How did you get it?" I asked.

"It wasn't just me, Anna. Everybody gave," Papa said. "All the Saints sent what they had. Seed money, wages, even monies saved to build homes so people wouldn't have to stay in shanties another year. Those men at Carthage don't know what they're up against. With the help of God, the Saints have come through." Papa laughed again, this time slapping his leg and leaning back in his chair.

"John," Mama said, trying to hide a smile.

Sidnie started laughing too, then jumped up from the table and ran around the table twice before Papa caught her up in his arms and hugged her tight.

The next afternoon we got word that Brother Joseph and Brother Hyrum hadn't even gotten out of Carthage before they were arrested and jailed again.

The bail money hadn't helped after all.

CHAPTER SEVEN

Brother Joseph

All day long I worked hard, trying to forget the Brethren in jail at Carthage. But I couldn't. I kept thinking what it might be like if Papa were taken from our family the same way Brother Joseph had been taken from his.

I wondered what it would be like to have to stay somewhere that was too hot or too cold. How would it feel to be in a place where maybe I couldn't get a drink when I wanted it, or where I couldn't get away? I wondered what it would be like to spend months away from home. For me, one night would be too long to be away from my family.

I remembered the times when Joseph Smith would come back after being imprisoned before. He always had things to teach the Saints. He received revelations from the Lord while in jail, revelations that he said offered comfort to him. He spoke to us of building a Zion community here in Nauvoo, living as God wished us to live. And for a while he had been safe here.

As I did my chores, hot in the afternoon, I wished for a melon cooled in the river. I wished I could take one to the Prophet.

When it was late, after supper and nearing time for bed, I crept up the stairs to my room. I went to the clothes press, took out my nightdress, and changed clothes. Then after a few minutes of trying to decide what to do, I took out my pad of paper and my drawing pencil. I just stood there holding my things, wanting to draw. If only I could I'd feel better sure. Drawing would get my mind off the Prophet.

Suddenly Charlette was in the doorway. "I'm telling," she said.

My pencil felt smooth and comfortable in my hand. My pad of paper was cool. I ignored Charlette. I stood there, not looking at my sister, thinking of the troubles that had followed us here to Nauvoo, wondering if we would ever be free of them.

"I'm telling, I say," said Charlette again.

I walked quietly across the room and looked out the window at the temple. The night was still. There were none of the usual sounds of building that could always be heard from the temple during the day, just calm. The evening seemed a lie. Things weren't really as peaceful as this night appeared. Our prophet was in jail.

I remembered back a few months before, when Brother Joseph came to give Mama a blessing about the baby she was carrying. He told Mama that this baby would be whole and well. After the blessing, we were sent to bed. But once Charlette and Sidnie were asleep, I crept out of bed and sat on the stairs to listen to my folks talk to the Prophet.

Brother Joseph said that he didn't think the persecution of the Saints was going to end here in Nauvoo. He thought we should leave. I knew I should have been frightened then, hearing him speak of traveling again, but his voice was so peaceful that I wasn't. I remembered him saying he knew we were supposed to go to the Rocky Mountains. He and Papa had talked late into the night, sitting near the fireplace, and I had sat quiet and hidden, while he spoke about another move west. Sister Emma didn't want to pack up again. And I could tell by looking at Mama's face, bright in the fire- and candlelight, that she didn't want to either. After our visitors left, Papa turned to Mama and said something I found curious.

"When the Prophet tells us to move on, we will."

Mama didn't say anything for a minute. "Of course, John. You know I wouldn't hesitate."

"There will be those that do."

Mama nodded then. I snuck quickly to my bed that night. I dreamed of walking again, remembering the long walk to Nauvoo. I dreamed of Mama crying when she left my little brother's grave behind.

A noise brought me back to my room and out of remembering. Charlette was standing in the door still, her hand covering her mouth, crying.

"What's the matter?" I asked.

Charlette ran forward and fell on the bed. She cried into the straw tick mattress.

"What's the matter?" I asked again. "Are you ailing? Do you have a pain somewhere? Do you need a dose of cod liver oil?"*

Charlette shook her head, her light curls bouncing, but never did she look at me.

"Then what are you crying about?"

"About Brother Joseph."

"Why?" I asked.

"He's in jail."

"He's been in jail before. Lots of times. Too many times."

"I'm missing him. That's why I'm crying. I don't want him there. I want him here, safe with us, in Nauvoo."

I sat a moment, then touched Charlette on her back. She was warm and so slight I could feel her bones. Her shoulders shook with sobs that she tried to make softer by crying into the mattress. It would never do for Mama or Papa to see her acting so. But somehow, all this crying joined my sister to me. I felt close to Charlette. I wanted to lie down beside her and cry, too.

Instead, I rubbed her back and said, "No crying now, Charlette Robinson. Brother Joseph would want us to be brave no matter what."

"But I'm not brave, Anna. Not like you. I'm scared."

"Nonsense," I said, surprised to hear what she thought of me. "Of course you are. And I'll let you in on a little secret. I'm not so brave after all. Now try not to cry."

Charlette sat up and held her breath to make her tears stop. Then she wiped her eyes. I put my arm around her. She seemed so frail. So little.

"There," I said. "You're doing it."

"But you *are* brave, Anna," Charlette said, sniffing a little. "You went to the river all alone. And in the dark, too."

"I don't know if that was what one would call brave," I said, laughing. "Why, Papa didn't think it was anything more than pure deviltry."

Charlette smiled at me. Then she hung her head. "I'm sorry, Anna, for telling Papa about your drawing. I don't know why I did it. You're always helping out so much. And Sidnie likes being with you better'n me and . . . and . . . I want to do something as good as you."

I squeezed Charlette close to me.

"Well, drawing isn't the right thing, sure," I said. "If I had only known . . . why Charlette, I would have sketched with you. Taught you all I know. But Papa has made the rule and we must follow it." I sighed and touched my pad of paper there on the bed beside us.

"Can I see what you've drawn, Anna?" Charlette asked. "I wouldn't blame you, not one bit, if you said I wasn't allowed." Charlette's chin was thrust forward in case I was going to say no.

"It will be hard to see here in the almost dark," I said. "And the moon's not up yet."

"I'll look real close."

I opened the school pad, and carefully, picture by picture I showed Charlette my drawings.

"Here's the temple, one late afternoon. Here's that old willow in Widow Smythe's yard. That's Brother Edward running the sawmill."

"Why it looks just like him, Anna."

"Here's Betsy with Papa milking her. And see the cat? He's waiting for a taste of milk."

"They look almost alive, Anna. I can't believe how good you draw."

"Well, I like doing it."

At the picture of the Prophet, Charlette breathed in deep. "Why, I can almost see that his eyes are blue, the likeness is so true. Show this to Mama, Anna. I think it would make her feel better. She's worried so."

"I can't. I made a promise to Papa and Mama. They're not wanting to see this." I closed the book and after a moment went and put it back in its hiding place.

"Prayer, girls," Papa called up the stairs.

Charlette came and stood near me. "I truly am sorry, Anna," she said. "I wish with all my heart I hadn't said a thing—that I could take it all back."

"Wouldn't it be nice to change things with just a

wish," I said. I was thinking about the men in Carthage. If I could, I would wish them free.

I hugged my sister tight then and we ran down the stairs for evening prayer. We were friends.

The next night I dreamed that someone was pounding on the door, angry because I had been drawing again. The pounding didn't stop, even when I sat up in bed. I was confused till I realized where I was.

"What is it?" Charlette asked."

"I'm scared," whimpered Sidnie. She put her tiny arms tight around my neck.

"Just someone at the door," I said. "Papa will take care of it."

Right then I heard Papa say something soft, to whoever was outside.

"You're needed, Brother John," a man said in a loud voice full of sorrow. "Sister Emma has asked for you. Brothers Joseph and Hyrum were shot in Carthage by a mob. The Prophet and his brother are dead."

CHAPTER EIGHT

MISSING THE PROPHET

I leapt from my place in bed and ran down the stairs, not even caring that I was in my nightclothes.

"Go back upstairs, Anna," Papa said. His voice sounded funny.

"Papa!" I threw myself into his arms. At his touch I started crying.

He hugged me only for a moment, then pulled away. "I can't stay here, Anna. I have to leave. I'm needed at the Smith home. Hurry up to your mother. I'm sure she has heard this news and it cannot be good for her." Papa kissed my forehead and left.

Brother Joseph, oh, Brother Joseph.

I turned to go back to bed. I wanted to crumple on the stairs, to fall where I was standing and not get back up. I wanted to cry till all my tears were gone. But I couldn't. It wasn't a brave thing to cry too much. It wasn't what Papa needed me to do. And I knew in my heart that it wasn't what the Prophet would want me to do.

Mama was on our bed with Charlette and Sidnie. Her face was pale in the candlelight. I could see her hands shaking. But her voice was calm.

"Anna, come get into bed. It's too late at night for you to worry. I can't have you catching the ague."*

"Papa said I should help you." I wiped my eyes on my hands but I couldn't stop myself from crying. Mama opened her arms to me and I ran over. I knelt on the floor next to her and put my head against her stomach. The baby was kicking hard. Mama smoothed my hair with her hand.

"Brother Joseph said this baby would be whole and well," I said between sobs.

"Yes, he did."

"I miss him already."

"So do I," Charlette said and she began to cry harder.

"He'll be back," said Sidnie.

Mama held me for a while. She spoke soothing words. At last I climbed back into bed. She tucked the light blanket down around us, then said a prayer in a voice so soft I could hardly hear it. She kissed us all and taking the candle, walked out of our room.

I didn't think I'd sleep, but somehow, I did.

The room was bright with the morning when I opened my eyes. Sidnie and Charlette slept soundly beside me. Something was weighing on my mind and I couldn't remember quite what it was. Then I did.

The Prophet is dead, I thought. My friend is dead. I whispered the words to see if saying them made believing this awful thing any easier. It didn't.

I got up slowly, not wanting to start the day. I had to *really* help Papa and Mama now. I dressed and tip-toed quietly from the room, leaving my sisters asleep.

Mama was sitting at the kitchen table when I walked into the room. The kitchen was already hot with the stove fire and the coming day. She ladled mush into a bowl for me, then poured on cream from yesterday's milk and a spoonful of sugar.

"You probably won't feel like it," Mama said, "but you'll be needing to eat all of this."

She was right. Breakfast tasted like sweetened dirt, gritty like the garden soil was when I accidently wiped it near my mouth, then touched its dryness with my tongue. It was hard to swallow because of the lump that was big in my throat.

"Will they be coming for us?" I asked.

"Who?" For a moment I thought I saw fear in Mama's eyes and it made my heart pound all the harder.

"The people that killed Brother Joseph and Brother Hyrum." It was hard to talk around the lump. It hurt. My heart hurt.

Mama looked at me, her eyes bluer than the sky. "I don't know, Anna," she said.

I went about my duties afraid. My stomach was cold with a fear that seemed to trickle down my backbone. I helped Mama so that she wouldn't have to do too much. She didn't look well. We all walked quietly with our mourning except for Sidnie, who didn't really know what was happening. She ran here and there until finally Mama made her sit in the parlor on a rocker. And then Sidnie cried, kicking her feet in a temper and rocking so hard I thought she would fall from the chair. Mama went to lie down.

I don't know how long it was before I heard the people in the streets. A great wailing filled the air as they marched past us.

"What is it?" I asked Papa, who had come in from town. "Where is everyone going?"

"To meet the Prophet and the Patriarch. Doctor Richards is bringing their bodies back today."

"I want to go," I said. And suddenly Mama and my sisters were standing in the room.

"We'll all go," said Mama.

"Lydia," Papa said. "Perhaps that's not wise. The baby."

Mama laid her hand softly on Papa's arm. "Last night Anna reminded me of Brother Joseph's blessing. This baby will live." She didn't wait for an answer but looked at us. "Go get your shoes on."

We joined the people walking through the streets. Men, women, and children went to meet the wagon. Some people were crying, others wailing. Some looked angry, some unbelieving. Everywhere, dogs were barking. We went east for nearly a mile and after waiting for only a short time, we heard someone call, "The wagons are coming."

The crowds parted, and the wagons that bore the bodies of our beloved Prophet and Patriarch rolled slowly past us. Then *everyone* began to cry. I had never heard such a sad noise in all my life. One lady fainted into her husband's arms. Mama bowed her head as the wagon passed. She stumbled and Papa held her up close.

"It's true," she said. "I was hoping, praying that perhaps they were still alive."

We closed in behind the wagons and followed them all the way to the Mansion House. We separated into families and walked back to our homes. Mama leaned on Papa the whole way. It took a great effort to get the chores done. To make supper. To get ready for bed. I wondered if everyone in Nauvoo was hurting as we were at this great loss.

When I thought my sisters were asleep, I crawled out of bed and went over to the window. The wind rustled in the chestnut tree—a warm breeze that just moved the mosquitoes around a bit.

"What are you doing?" Charlette said soft-like from the bed.

"Thinking," I said.

"About Brother Joseph?"

"Yes. And something I heard Papa say a long time ago."

"What?" Charlette sniffed and I knew that she was crying still.

"I heard him tell Mama that if Brother Joseph told us to leave Nauvoo and go further west, that we would go right then. I was wondering if we will leave now that this has happened."

Charlette was quiet for a time. I thought maybe she had gone back to sleep when she asked, "What do *you* figure we'll do?"

I breathed in deep. "Whatever the Lord tells us, I guess."

I stood at the window awhile longer, worrying about what tomorrow, and the day after, and the day after that would bring us now that our Prophet was dead.

CHAPTER NINE

Drawing for Myself

We waited until the chores were done and our breakfast eaten before we went to pay last respects to Brother Joseph and Brother Hyrum. I had cried so much the night before that I was sure my eyes were dry. But when we got to the Mansion House and I saw everyone else there so brokenhearted I became weepy all over again. Not Mama. She stood straight and tall, holding on to Papa only a little. Her face was grim and her lips were in a straight line. There were so many people waiting that I knew we would be in line for a long while before we told Joseph and Hyrum Smith good-bye.

The air was damp. The trees looked dark green. The sky was gray with a coming storm. Every once in a while the wind gusted in, raising dust and making the trees and bushes bow before it. There was little relief from the heat.

As we stood waiting to enter the brick building Brother Joseph had been so proud of, I listened to the people around me. Some of the men were angry. They said if the Nauvoo Legion still had their guns, they could ride into Carthage and clear the place of the mob that was responsible for the deaths of the men we most revered.

"Let's go with what we have," someone said. "We can take clubs and sticks and pitchforks, if necessary. And we have our own firearms." A few people spoke up in agreement.

"They think killing Joseph Smith will break us all up," I heard another man say. "But they're wrong. The truth will continue strong until the Lord comes again. Justice will be served."

"Let's hurry justice along. We'll make those blood-thirsty heathens pay for what they have done."

Suddenly Papa started talking. "Brethren, do you think the Lord would want us to take revenge?"

"They've pushed us from Kirtland to here," a tall, angry man in the crowd said. "My wife died on the trail to Nauvoo. Now our Prophet is gone. If we keep on this way, we'll never find a place to settle in peace."

"Brother," Papa said. His voice was quiet. "There

isn't a family here that hasn't been touched with sorrow. Especially today. But we cannot take matters into our own hands. We must wait and see what the Lord would have us do."

We can't let them keep doing this to us," the tall man said.

"We have to follow the Lord. That's what makes us different from the mobs who persecute us. Do you wish to be as they are?"

The man was silent. "You're right," he said at last, his head bowed. "I'll wait to see what the Brethren say we should do."

I looked at Papa. He and Brother Joseph had been so close. I could tell by his face that he was deeply pained by all that had happened. I felt proud that he was able to think of doing what was right, even though things were so bad now.

The line moved slowly. One kindly woman offered us her place in line when she saw Mama's condition.

At long last we were in the house and making our way to the coffins. My eyes filled with tears and I could not bring myself to look upon Joseph and Hyrum Smith.

Mama, who was ahead of me, took a few steps

past where the Prophet and Patriarch lay. Then looking back at Papa, her face pale, she said, "Get Sister Eliza. This baby is coming."

Papa scooped Mama up, even though she protested, and left the room. His boots made loud thumps on the wooden floor. And I hurried off, Charlette and Sidnie following behind me, to find Sister Eliza, who would help Mama with the baby.

It was a little boy, so small and red and wrinkled that I nearly laughed with the joy of it.  He cried when anyone but Mama held him, but I didn't mind. Mama kept him in the bed with her, letting him sleep beside her, instead of in the tiny cradle Papa had built years ago when I was born. It stood empty. And for once the emptiness didn't mean anything bad.

At dinner, four days after the baby was born, Papa told us that Mama had decided to name the baby Joseph Hyrum Robinson and he hoped we were all in agreement with it. We all were, except for Sidnie who kept on wanting to call him Sarah. Even after we explained that we needed a boy's name and not a girl's, Sidnie stuck her lip out and mumbled, "Well, I'll call him Sarah. And I say he'll like it, too."

As happy as Mama was about baby Joseph, she was still sad about Brother Joseph's dying. At times I wondered if she'd ever be comforted.

"If I just had something to remember him by," she often said, especially when she was really tired.

"You have baby Joseph," Papa would say. "And the things in your heart."

"Yes," Mama said. "You're right John, of course. But sometimes I feel that if I could just see the Prophet's face one more time, my heart would not ache so."

Charlette stared at me in a funny way one afternoon when we heard Papa and Mama talking this way for at least the hundredth time. We were outside their room, where Mama was still resting and would be until the baby was six weeks old.

"Why are you looking at me so queerly?" I asked Charlette, carrying the tray of dishes down to be washed.

Charlette just stood quiet, then shook her head at me. Her long curls bounced around her shoulders.

After doing the dishes I went to work in the garden. Seeing the melons made my throat hurt. How I wished

I had been able to carry one to Brother Joseph.

"Anna," Charlette said from the back door, "Papa and Mama want to see you up in their room."

I dusted my hands on the skirt of my dress and followed my sister upstairs. "Is anything wrong?" I asked. Suddenly I was worried about little Joseph. "Is it the baby?" I pushed Charlette aside and ran past her.

Papa was holding the tiny bundle and sitting next to Mama on the bed. Mama had my drawing paper in her hands. I stopped in the doorway. I couldn't make myself move a step more. Mama was crying. Charlette came up close behind me. I looked at my sister. She told on me again! I couldn't believe it.

"Papa! Mama!" I said, trying to keep my voice low because of the baby. "I haven't drawn since you told me not to. I promise." It seemed so long ago that I had held my drawing paper and pencil.

"This likeness is perfect," Mama said, her eyes round with surprise. "It looks just like Joseph Smith."

"You have a true talent, little one," Papa said.

For a second I could hear Brother Joseph telling me that I had a gift for drawing. I could see him standing tall in the hot June sunlight, smiling down at me.

"We were wrong to tell you not to draw," Mama said.

"What?" I asked. Could I be hearing them right?

"Mama so wanted something to remind her of Brother Joseph," Charlette said. "I remembered your drawing and knew that it would be perfect for her."

"Come close, Anna," Mama said, beckoning me with her fingers. I walked to where she sat propped up in bed and took her hand.

"Anna, may I set this up in my room until I am feeling better?" Mama showed me the picture of the Prophet that I had drawn the day he had played marbles. It seemed so long ago now.

"Of course," I said. "I'd be proud for you to."

I walked around the bed and without touching him with my dirty hands, kissed baby Joseph. When I looked up, Charlette was grinning at me so big I thought her face might break in half.

"Why are you looking at me like that?" I asked, but I couldn't help smiling back.

"Mama told me it would be all right if you taught me to draw like you do."

"What?" My voice went up high and Mama put her finger to her lips to hush me.

"You can draw, Anna!" said Charlette, clapping her hands together softly. Sidnie who sat close to Mama, laughed.

I looked from Mama to Papa.

"Yes, little one," Papa said. "You can draw. As long as your chores are done. I cannot restrict you after seeing what you can do."

I couldn't say anything. I just stared at Papa and Mama. I could draw again! I wanted to shout it to the sky, loud so that everyone could hear.

"Are you forgetting your manners?" asked Mama.

"Oh, Papa," I said. I hugged him as best I could with the baby in his arms. "Thank you! Thank you both!"

Before the sun set, after all the chores were done, I had Mama sit up in the bed with baby Joseph.

"Smile," I said.

"Anna, do you think it's dignified to smile in a portrait?"

"Of course, Mama. You're happy aren't you?"

Mama nodded at me. "As happy as can be expected."

"Act as if I'm not here. That way we'll get a picture that looks most like you."

Mama looked down at baby Joseph and smiled.

I started drawing.

GLOSSARY
In Anna's own words:

ague (pg. 51)–The ague was a sickness that struck the Saints when we first moved to Nauvoo. We thought the sickness came from breathing the night swamp air, but it was really spread by mosquitoes. Once we were able to drain the land, the fever and shaking that we called ague did not occur as often because there was no place for the mosquitoes to breed.

clothes press (pg. 10)–My clothes press was just a place I kept my clothing, like a closet.

cod liver oil (pg. 45)–Medical doctors were rarely depended upon in the 1800s. Often when I got sick, Mama would take care of me, sometimes making me take a big spoonful of nasty tasting cod liver oil to make me better.

"A lot of the **fences** are down and the wheat is gone" (pg. 7)–When Brother Joseph set up the city of Nauvoo, he did it so that we would be closer to one another for social and spiritual reasons. The town was a little like a wagon wheel, with crops on the outside of town and people in the center.

". . . **firing** cannons" (pg. 28)–If anyone was feared to have drowned, the paddleboats would go up and down the river, shooting cannons in hopes of loosening the body if it was caught on a tree limb underwater so it would float to the top.

frittering (pg. 5)–When Papa said I was frittering away time, he thought I was wasting time.

milliner (pg. 14)–A milliner is a person who makes hats. Mama really loved hats and would always shop at the milliner's store.

moccasin (pg. 24)–Sometimes called a water moccasin or cottonmouth, a moccasin is a snake that lives near the water. Its poison is very deadly and this snake has been known to actually attack other living things, including people.

". . . it was a huge amount of **money**" (pg. 40)– In 1844, $7,500 was an enormous amount of money. Mama could buy one dozen eggs for five cents, and a man could work hard all day long and only make a dollar. We didn't have a lot of money. Mostly we bartered or traded goods for what we needed, so you can see that the bail that was set for the Prophet and the other Brethren was a large amount.

plaited (pg. 29)–When I plaited my hair I was braiding it.

sacrament cup (pg. 12)–When the sacrament was passed, we drank from one common glass instead of tiny paper cups. And all the men and boys sat on one side of the room and all the women and girls and babies sat on the other, as we did in school.

". . . in my best **script**" (pg. 9)–Script means handwriting. Good penmanship was important to me. I worked hard to make sure that my script was easy to read and pretty to look at.

spectacles (pg. 12)–Spectacles is an old-fashioned way of saying glasses.

"**. . . strands** that caught in the comb" (pg. 29)– One of the hobbies of the girls and women of my time was doing embroidery. We would save the strands of hair that came loose when we brushed our hair and make embroidered samplers, using our hair as thread.

temple (pg. 16)–When we first moved to Nauvoo and construction began on our temple, many people did not have money to give as tithing. In order for us to pay a full and honest tithe, we gave a tenth of our garden produce. Papa also tithed his time, working one day out of ten on the temple.

trousers (pg. 2)–Trousers is another name for boys' pants.

wash tub (pg. 29)–Usually Mama would heat water on the stove or over a fire in the fireplace for us to bathe in and get clean for our Sunday meeting. We didn't have any running water in the house. We had to get it from the well and then heat it. If there wasn't time to let a big pot of water get warm, baths in the wash tub were cold. Brrr!

Author's Note:

Back in the 1800s it was considered an idle practice for people to draw or act in plays. Even reading anything other than the scriptures was often considered a waste of time. A family had to get their crops harvested and take care of themselves in order to survive. Brother and Sister Robinson were not trying to be mean to their daughter Anna. They wanted her to be wise and able to take care of her own family when she grew up. If she had wasted too much time drawing, it could be bad for all of them.

What Really Happened

Anna and her family are just a creation of the author's imagination. But there are many true parts to this story.

Joseph Smith really did live in Nauvoo in 1844. He and his older brother Hyrum were martyred on June 27 of that very year. A mob of about 100 men, many with their faces painted black so no one would know who they were, stormed the jail in Carthage to kill the Prophet.

Hyrum was killed first. Joseph went to the window and was shot dead.

Joseph and Hyrum were not alone that day. Willard Richards and John Taylor were with them. Dr. Richards and John Taylor both lived. Brother Taylor was severely wounded, but he later became the third prophet of the Church.

About the Author

Carol Lynch Williams loves to write—especially for girls. She is not certain if that's because she is a girl (an older girl, yes) or because she has four daughters and would like more daughters. She and her husband, Drew, live with their family in Mapleton, Utah.

Carol joined the Church when she was seventeen, along with her sister, Samantha. Her sister has always been her very good friend.

When Carol was twenty-two years old she went on a mission to North Carolina and was called to work with deaf people. She really enjoyed working with the hearing impaired. It was in the mission field that she learned many important things that have helped her throughout her life.

At this writing Carol has two other books published with Delacorte Press, and several others in process.

More about
The Latter-day Daughters Series

After reading Anna's story be sure to enjoy the other books in the Latter-day Daughters Series. They are about girls just like you who lived in other times and places. Read about Clarissa, who had to leave everything to come to America; Laurel, who braved the frightening days at Haun's Mill; Maren, who discovered a brand new way to be happy—and watch for many more! These stories of adventure, laughter, tears, and fun have been written just for you.